Jack and Rick

Jack and Rick

David McPhail

Green Light Readers
Harcourt, Inc.
San Diego   New York   London

Requests for permission to make copies of any part of the work should be mailed
to the following address: Permissions Department, Harcourt, Inc.,
6277 Sea Harbor Drive, Orlando, Florida 32887-6777.

www.harcourt.com

First Green Light Readers edition 2002
Green Light Readers is a trademark of Harcourt, Inc.,
registered in the United States of America and/or other jurisdictions.

Library of Congress Cataloging-in-Publication Data
McPhail, David M.
Jack and Rick/David McPhail.
p. cm.
"Green Light Readers."
Summary: Jack and Rick want to play together, but there's a river
between them and they will have to work together to bridge it.
[1. Cooperativeness—Fiction. 2. Friendship—Fiction.] I. Title. II. Series.
PZ7.M2427Jac 2002
[E]—dc21   2001002369
ISBN 0-15-216552-5
ISBN 0-15-216540-1 (pb)

A C E G H F D B
A C E G H F D B (pb)

Jack and Rick want to play.

Can Jack pick up the log?

No, it's too big!

Can Rick help Jack?

Yes, Rick can pass the rope.

Can they lift it now?

Yes, they can.

Can Rick walk to Jack?

No! Oh no!

Can Jack help Rick?

Yes, Jack can help.

Now, Jack and Rick can play.

Meet the Author-Illustrator

David McPhail loves the way Jack and Rick work together as a team. He says, "I like the way the characters in this story find a way to get on the same side of the stream—even though it's not easy." He hopes you help your friends the way Jack and Rick helped each other!

David McPhail